My Grandfather's Hat

WRITTEN AND ILLUSTRATED BY KEIKO NARAHASHI

I HAVE A FRIEND

ALSO ILLUSTRATED BY KEIKO NARAHASHI

THE LITTLE BAND by James Sage
RAIN TALK by Mary Serfozo
WHO SAID RED? by Mary Serfozo
WHO WANTS ONE? by Mary Serfozo
(Margaret K. McElderry Books)

My Grandfather's Hat

By Melanie Scheller
Illustrated by Keiko Narahashi

Margaret K. McElderry Books
New York

Maxwell Macmillan Canada
Toronto

Maxwell Macmillan International
New York   Oxford   Singapore   Sydney

For John Phillip Medlin
and for John Plymale
in honor of their grandfathers
—M.S.

For Peter, Micah, and Joy
—K.N.

Text copyright © 1992 by Melanie Scheller
Illustrations copyright © 1992 by Keiko Narahashi

Margaret K. McElderry Books
Macmillan Publishing Company
866 Third Avenue
New York, NY 10022

Maxwell Macmillan Canada, Inc.
1200 Eglinton Avenue East
Suite 200
Don Mills, Ontario M3C 3N1

Macmillan Publishing Company is part of the Maxwell Communication Group of Companies.
First edition
Printed in Hong Kong
10 9 8 7 6 5 4 3 2 1
The text of this book is set in Hanover.
The illustrations are rendered in watercolor and pencils.

Library of Congress Catalog Card Number: 91-12486
ISBN 0-689-50540-X

My grandfather was supposed to hang his hat on the coatrack when he came to visit, but sometimes he forgot and left it on the sofa. I'm not supposed to bounce on the sofa, but sometimes I forget. One day when I jumped on the sofa, I landed on my grandfather's hat and squashed it flat.

"Jason!" my mother said. "Just look what you've done to your grandfather's hat."

"Now, Susie, leave the boy alone." Susie is what my grandfather called my mother. My dad calls her Susan.

My grandfather put the hat on my head and pulled it over my ears. The hat made a *plock* sound, and when Grandpa took it off my head, it looked the way it did before I jumped on it. My mother looked like she was going to say something, but instead she shook her head and went into the kitchen. When she was gone, my grandfather winked at me and tickled my belly button.

My grandfather bought his hat seventeen years ago, a long time before I was born. He said back then they built things to last. He had a lawn mower that was twelve years old and a car that was twenty years old. He told me I could drive the car when I grow up.

When my grandfather and I went for a walk and he saw someone
he knew, he'd lift his hat off his head and hold it there for a second.
He'd nod his head one time and say, "Mornin'." Then he'd put the
hat back on his head.

Last year my grandfather and I built a snowman. Grandpa told me that in the old days people used pieces of coal to make eyes and mouths for their snowmen. We didn't have any coal, so we used some pickles that my grandfather brought from the kitchen. We ate all the pickles that were left.

My grandfather put his hat on the snowman's head. Then we built a little snowman next to the big one and put my baseball cap on it.

My grandfather said, "The big one's middle looks like mine," and he patted his stomach. My grandmother always called Grandpa's stomach a potbelly.

Once my grandfather carried a dozen eggs home from the chicken house in his hat. One of them broke and made a big mess in his hat.

When my grandmother saw what had happened, she said, "Wilson! Your best hat!"

"I guess the yolk's on me," he told her. He told me that was a joke called a pun and that I would understand it when I was older. He wiped the hat clean and put it back on his head.

My grandfather died two months ago. My dad says Grandpa
can't be with us anymore, but our memories of him will always be
with us. Now my grandmother lives with us.

My mother had a yard sale and sold my grandfather's lawn mower. My father sold my grandfather's car to a man who said it was in mint condition. But Grandma gave my grandfather's hat to me. She said Grandpa would have wanted me to have it.

"Now remember, Jason, you're not to wear that hat," my mother told me. "It's a keepsake, not a toy."

My grandmother said, "Oh, Susan, let him wear it. There's nothing he can do to it that your father hasn't done already."

I'm glad I have my grandfather's hat. Sometimes I hold the hat over my head and look at myself in the mirror. I nod my head one time and say, "Mornin'."

It's too big for me now, but someday, when I grow up, I will wear my grandfather's hat.